EVICTION MY ASS

A NOVEL BY
NABILA GERON

FOR EVERYONE WHO BELIEVE IN ME.

The will of God will never take you to where the grace of God will not protect you. To gain that which is worth having, it may be necessary to lose everything else.
#BLESSEDTOBEABLESSING

The year was 2015. The morning was average, unlike most mornings as the hazy sun came spilling in through the cracks in the curtains. Calista woke up to fix her husband's breakfast before he went to work, a ritual she'd gotten used to over the past ten years. She was already dressed and had coffee brewing when her husband got up from bed. Dressing and showering, he ate breakfast with a smile and some quiet conversation. He then finished his coffee and kissed Calista on the cheek before leaving the house.

Calista stood by the door for a few moments after her husband left, staring out into the empty hallway. She has been doing this for nearly a decade now, ever since she married him in fact; just standing there at the door, staring out into nothingness after he left for work. And every day was the same thing: good morning kiss on the cheek, being served breakfast in bed by Calista while she was already dressed and ready to go with coffee brewing, a quick shower while Calista set his lunch box on the table, eating breakfast with small talk and smiles all around before downing his coffee and kissing her again before leaving for work.

But today was different; even though everything seemed normal on the outside, Calista felt uneasy inside. She couldn't put her finger on what was wrong, but something had changed. Maybe it was the way that he kissed her this morning? She shrugged it off and went about her day.

Average, normal as it is every weekday. Calista woke her children up and dressed the younger ones to go to school. After a breakfast of eggs, fruit, and muffins, they grabbed bags, shoes, and jackets to walk to school. She always walked them to school, which was three blocks away past the local bodegas, markets, and the multiple apartment buildings in the neighborhood. Nothing unusual as she dropped them off at the front door of the school.

Calista went home, unremarkably getting into the swing of her daily routine. She hadn't even noticed it in the past five years, perfecting her routine. She started with doing laundry, cleaning in between loads in the dryer and on their balcony. She would be cleaning up the apartment and watching TV, game shows, talk shows, and usually some sort of drama or soap opera. Being a housewife and a stay-at-home mom was her life and she finished washing, folding, and storing laundry before cleaning the small sink of dishes. Nothing unusual.

The sun had come out that day and it was blue past the haze and noise of the neighborhood around her. However, what was unusual was that her husband, Jeff, hadn't called to tell her what time he'd be home. It varied week by week but some nights he was home at five, others he wasn't home until well after seven. She was a bit worried when three came and went and she had to go get her children soon.

So, Calista picked up the phone to call her husband's workplace. His boss, whom she'd met at Christmas parties, summers in the park, and at a few birthdays, told her that he didn't show up for work. Panic had set in, and Calista was getting worried, picking up her children from school in as calm, in a way as possible. She did not want to alarm them if there was no need.

However, when she got home from picking them up and got the eldest working on their homework, she had become distracted by their daily routine after school. It was hard to break from the routine as the youngest insisted she could go to the concrete park shared by the local apartment buildings. Calista couldn't indulge her and thought maybe something bad had happened. Shortly before dinner, as the simple pasta and meat dish simmered, the phone rang, and Calista answered it.

The moment she answered the call, her stomach dropped. Without knowing what would be said by the other person on the line, she had a deeply gut-wrenching feeling that something was wrong. She took a deep breath and cleared her throat of the lump that had formed in it and then said, "Hello."

The woman was on the other end, her voice unfamiliar, but she spoke with conviction and a coldness that Calista didn't understand.

"Jeff isn't coming home. So, don't report him missing," she spoke, a crackling buzz between them. "He's safe but he's done, and you need to accept that."

"I don't understand," Calista replied, even though the picture had suddenly become crystal clear. Still, she refused to believe that Jeff had been unfaithful to her until she heard it from his lips.

"Don't play dumb," the woman scoffed, "he told you he was going on a business trip almost every weekend. Any smart woman knows what that means."

She wasn't wrong. However, Calista was so set on her daily routine and keeping the family functioning that she chose to block out the fact that her husband was gone every other weekend.

"May I speak to him?" Calista asked, keeping her temper under wraps.

A long pause stood between them and then Jeff got on the phone.

"There's nothing to say," Jeff said, his voice somber but steady.

"Nothing at all?"

"We talked three years ago when Jean was born," he said, Calista recalling a heated conversation. Jean was the youngest and their fifth child.

At the time, she had been struggling with postpartum depression and thought their fight was just from the tension in the house. Raising five kids was not easy, especially in Los Angeles, and they all survived on Jeff's income alone. She knew it was hard for him to take care of all the bills alone, and a part of her felt guilty that her acting career had never taken flight.

"I don't understand, you're just abandoning us?" she asked him, already knowing what his response would be. Jeff was not someone who changed his mind. He always thought things through. Which meant he had thought and planned this for a very long time.

"I can't live like that anymore; I'm not coming back. Don't look for me," he said, his voice still cold and steady. "Good luck."

He hung up, the silence hanging in the air as her eldest, Tia, stirred the pasta dish and drained the broccoli in the sink. She was almost eleven and she was already adept at helping with her siblings, housework, school, and cooking on her own. Calista was proud but ashamed that her daughter had to learn all these things at such a young age. As she hung up the squawking phone, watching Tia, she knew things were about to get a lot harder.

To Calista, Jeff was everything. He was the man she had fallen for in college, the father of her five beautiful children, and a constant presence in her life. He was the rock that held them together; he was the foundation of their family. He was working for the telephone company, as a telephone collector. His duties were to receive payment and post amount to customer's account, preparing statements to credit department if customer fails to respond, initiating repossession proceedings or service disconnection, and keeping records of collection and status of accounts.

Jeff is gone. She couldn't believe it. The worst part was that she wasn't surprised. After all, they'd already talked about this three years ago when Jean was born—a conversation that she remembered as being particularly heated. But now he was really gone, and she knew her life was about to get a lot harder. Calista put the phone in the receiver and just sat there for some time, letting the shock wash over her as she tried to imagine what she would do next. Jeff had been her partner for so long—how could he just leave her like this?

After dinner, she spoke with Tia and her only son, nine-year-old Duane. She wasn't sure how to explain it to them, but she kept her emotions in check, explaining their father had left and wasn't coming back. She explained that he wasn't happy and that she didn't know he was planning to do this. She also told them that things would get harder, from here on out, and that if they needed to talk about anything, she'd always hear their side of the story. Her kids were her world, but explaining this concept to Irene and Jennifer, her other two daughters who just started kindergarten and first grade, was going to be harder.

The next morning at breakfast, Irene was sitting at the table with her head in her hands. She asked Calista if something was wrong with daddy? Why did daddy leave? What did daddy mean when he said he wouldn't be coming back?

It took all of Calista's might for her not to cry. Instead, she explained that their father had left because he was unhappy—and unhappy people don't make good parents.

The walk home from her children's school was different the next day. All Calista could think about was the dreaded phone call the night before. All she could hear was Jeff's words confirming that he had abandoned her and their five children.

On the surface, Jeff had seemed like a great husband and father. He worked hard at a stable job to provide for his family, and he helped with chores around the house. He was successful in all aspects of life but one: when it came to his relationship with Calista, he would turn into a selfish child who felt entitled to everything without having to contribute anything himself.

When Calista first met Jeff, her friends thought she was crazy to get involved with him. They warned her that he would hurt her, but she didn't believe them... until now. Jeff left Calista holding the bag and taking care of all the responsibilities that came with raising five kids on her own.

She had sort of never worked outside of the home because Jeff was adamant that he wanted a wife who would stay at home and make sure their children were cared for without any outside help or interference. Now he wasn't even going to be there to take care of them himself! What are you going to do? Calista thought to herself as she trudged along.

The days that followed were filled with endless tears and endless questions from the kids. The only thing Calista was sure of was that if Jeff didn't come back, she needed to find a way to make ends meet, fast.

When she opened the door, she found a mess: dishes piled high in the sink, dust covering every surface, and all her children's toys thrown around haphazardly. She sighed. There was no one to help her clean those dishes or pick up those toys—no job to bring in money to pay for a housekeeper or a nanny.

She made her way to the kitchen to make herself some tea in order to escape the sadness of it all, but when she opened her tea cabinet, there was nothing there. Tears welled up in her eyes—how would she get through this without tea?

Calista spent the rest of the day feeling defeated and empty inside. She thought back to all those great times with Jeff and their children and wondered what had gone wrong between them.

As if things couldn't get any worse, the usual sunny Los Angeles sky was suddenly filled with thick dark clouds that threatened to break open at any given moment. Calista didn't have the energy to walk any faster. Her heart was as heavy as the clouds above. Overnight, she became a single mother with no job. She could barely afford to feed herself and her kids, let alone make rent and pay for daycare while she looked for employment.

She had heard about a new program called Unemployed Moms that was providing free daycare for mothers in her same situation. The thought of having free daycare gave Calista hope that she would be able to find a job soon and take care of her children again. But when she got to the address listed on the website for Unemployed Moms, there was nothing there, but a vacant lot filled with rubble and trash.

After buying a box of green tea from 99¢ store, Calista sat down on a bench next to the lot and cried softly into her hands until it began to rain. An orange bus pulled up alongside her, but Calista didn't even look up until the driver opened his door and hopped out. He asked if she needed help getting somewhere dry, but all Calista could do was shake her head no as more tears rolled down her cheeks. It almost never rained in LA, but of course, even the weather was against her.

The hardest part of all of it was that her kids needed her more than ever—and she just didn't know how she was going to be able to give them everything they needed.

Calista talked with her friend in her living room, serving her a glass of tea. It had only been a few days since Jeff had left and so far, she had heard nothing. He even quit his job, which made her situation dire. What little money they had in savings and checking could have been taken by him at any moment and so immediately, Calista went to the ATM. She had done so the night she had last spoken to him, Tia watching the kids as Calista went up the block to the bank. She withdrew the entire checking amount, $1,256.00 cash from the checking.

Calista had annoyed the teller as she came in only fifteen minutes before they closed their office. However, she also got out all her savings, transferring them to her own, new, savings account Jeff couldn't touch. She made sure of it, no one has access to this account but her. She'd get the debit card for her account in a week or two, but in the days that followed, she had to call up all her utility bills to make sure they were all in her name. By the time her friend had come over, everything but the apartment was in her name.

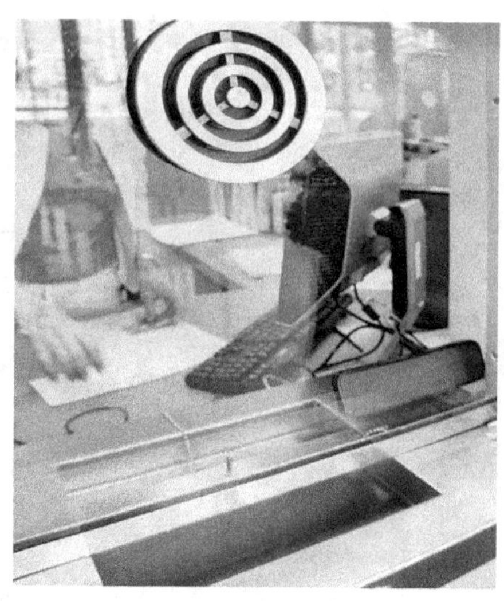

At first, Calista was too afraid to tell anyone what had happened, but after a few weeks, the news got out and people began to ask her about it. They would ask how she was doing, or if she needed anything, but Calista kept pushing them away. She didn't want their pity.

The only person who really helped her was her best friend Lynn, who came to her side during this difficult time. Lynn had been through a similar situation with her own ex-husband, and she told Calista that she had been through that pain before and came out on the other side of it stronger than ever before.

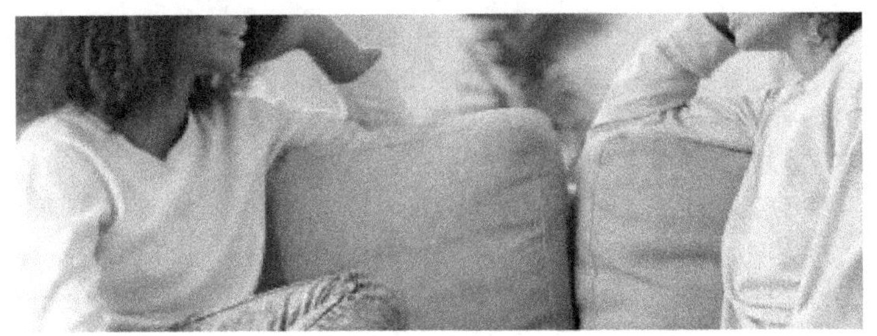

She was able to help Calista realize what she needed to do next. First, she told Calista not to panic, that everything was going to be okay. It was so important for her to hear that from someone she trusted.

Lynn didn't judge Calista or tell her that what Jeff did was okay; instead, she held her hand through the difficult days ahead and helped her avoid making any decisions that would make things worse for herself or the kids in the long run.

"Can I file for child support if I can't find the father?" Calista asked, trying to finally relax as the eldest was at school and baby Jean was napping in the room she shared with Tia.

"Yes, and you should," Lynn answered, sipping her tea as calmly as possible. She was just as angry as Calista wanted to be. "Until he is located, he cannot be served papers, and the child support will not begin to build up until there is a court hearing, under most circumstances."

"Most circumstances," she groaned, setting the tea down.

"My children's father was impossible for the state to find, and they had lots more in terms of resources than I or my lawyer did," Lynn explained, letting out her anger in her tone, trying to keep as quiet as possible so the three-year-old Jean wouldn't wake.

"I gave them his social security number, but there were no records of automobiles, tickets, incarcerations, employment, bank accounts, leases, utility bills, or tax returns. Nothing."

"Great…"

"Eventually, a woman he was involved with found me in a people search after they broke up, and she gave me a serviceable address ten years later," Lynn laughed, shaking her head. "A support order was in place before he disappeared, so it was still in force and all child support is owed."

"So, you are saying that it is only a matter of time until he is found and that until then, I'll just have to stick it out?"

"Exactly, get a lawyer, get a hold of social services, and get yourself a job," Lynn nodded, motioning around her. "You have a nice home and a great set of kids, Calista. Get some help when you need it. That is what it is for."

Calista took her children to social services that next day, excusing them from school. The children sat on the armless seats while their mom stood in the long line for an hour. Tia and Duane were mature enough to watch their three siblings. Calista finally made it up to the window, asking for food stamps and other financial assistance in hopes that her situation, when it came to child support, would get solved here.

Thankfully, it had been a simple but long process. She was given a case worker, access to food, rent, utility, and cash assistance as well as filing a child support claim against Jeff. She told her social worker what happened, and the woman genuinely seemed concerned and willing to help. It was also nice that they could cover half her rent until she found a steady job and childcare. Tia insisted she be homeschooled and look after Jean but that just wasn't going to happen, because Tia was 10 and Jean was 3.

As time passed, it's 2018, Calista had to cut back on her spending. She stopped buying name-brand foods and had to turn to store-brand goods instead. But she was still struggling, especially with the rent being so expensive. Her five kids were in the grocery store with her one night, and her youngest daughter Jean started to scream for OREO cookies, as many six-year-olds would do. Calista looked at her kids, who weren't happy at all about any of this. She wanted them to be happy and yet she was struggling with her low-level sales job and unable to give them everything they needed. That night, Calista just had enough.

She smiled at Jean and the others and said: "Okay, get whatever you want —we can afford to splurge this once." And splurge they did—filling up their cart with every kind of snack they could find: Cheetos and chips and soda and candy bars and even chocolate pudding cups with tiny plastic spoons that came in their own little cardboard box.

At the self-checkout, she scanned all of the food; paid half with cash and used food stamps for the rest; then bagged it all up with help from her oldest two children. They walked out of the store with bags in their hands and an exciting buzz about them. Those passing by them were curious and watching but she didn't care because her kids were happy at that moment—and that's really it.

Calista needed to do all she could to cut costs. Living in Los Angeles was very expensive for single people, but she had to do it earning minimum wage and with five kids. Each day, she felt as though the prices were rising and her bills were mounting. It began to feel unbearable. Calista was at her wit's end. She'd tried everything she could think of to manage her bills, but the expenses of life in Los Angeles were just too much for a minimum wage single mom to handle. As she came home from work, she began to feel like she was running out of options fast. With the rent being so high for a three-bedroom apartment and all of the other bills she couldn't afford to pay, having a car was useless.

Asking her uncle who was living in Carson, California to allow her to park her car on his driveway, because she couldn't afford the parking lot fee at her apartment was the next step in cutting back. She could walk to the grocery store and walk her kids to school, not really needing the car, her work just a short bus ride away. Los Angeles' commute transportations was easier. Bus stops were on every corner, metro train stations were not far.

She could go anywhere without any problem, and it would be over $100 a month cheaper. The bus driver would sometimes allow her and the kids to ride free. But at the train station, it would be hard to avoid the police who would check to see if anyone paid their ticket to ride the subway train. That's the last thing she would want, a fine ticket. Having food stamps and welfare checks weren't enough to pay the high rent nor was her minimum wage cashier job.

Sometimes Calista would go to her uncle's house to pick up the car and she would love to drive by La Santa Clarita and see people film movies. She got really excited about that and she hoped that one day she was going to be on one of those huge sets doing that same thing.

She thought about moving her and her kids into her friend's RV which was parked next to their house, but she didn't want to do that. She felt uneasy to depend on people to help her. She wished she could be able to pay for apartment rent on her own and a chance to at least use her acting skill to work on set.

A man named Nathaniel was hitting on her at the apartment's lobby. That was the last thing she needed to deal with a man. Nathaniel would probably be a good stepfather and could provide for her, but he's a chauffeur, claiming loudly and boisterously that he would make $4,000 a month. She didn't believe him, but it didn't matter because she wasn't ready for a love relationship. She wanted to be independent and to only focus on her children, taking care of them and their futures. She will not marry someone in the hope to bail her out. She wanted her husband to come back and do the right thing. Such as paying child support but so far, after three years, nothing has happened. No news of him or child support, to the annoyance of her caseworker.

At the end of every week, when she looked at her paycheck and her bank account, she was often left wondering how she had ended up like this. She felt that she was a good person, and she had worked hard all of her life. It just didn't seem right that someone should have to live like this, much less someone with children.

Calista knew that others were in the same boat as well. She could see it in the faces of those who lived there, or the conversations which would occur on the bus, or at the grocery store.

But even though she knew that speaking out was important, she also knew that there were many who might not understand what they were going through. There were those who would look down on people like her for being in this situation. They would judge them for not having enough money to make ends meet, or they might think they were lazy or stupid for not planning for divorce.

She searched for an apartment in California which she could pay $900 a month as she paid years ago, but things changed, the rent was ridiculous and very challenging. Her rent increased faster than the government welfare funds as well, making it impossible to make do with what was left over. They didn't go hungry but after rent came out of her paycheck, she was lucky to be able to afford clothes, soaps, and necessities.

Calista wanted to move out of her apartment, but the rent in other places was just as high. She had lived in this apartment for so long that it felt like home—she didn't want to move away from that feeling even though the place was worn down, but she needed a cheaper apartment very fast.

The apartment owner was also breathing down her neck, constantly renovating the building, waiting for her and her kids to move out so that they can increase the rent twice as much, over $1200 a month. They stopped having the maintenance to fix her toilet and other carpet cleaning services they used to provide. The carpet was getting black smog from California's dirty air and use. It was a nightmare she couldn't afford on top of plumbing and small appliance maintenance.

She could never afford to move to somewhere close-by and decent, with more than one bedroom, and this was a constant problem. She had to find a better-paying job or multiple jobs. However, what she was doing was paying her neighbor, a poor college-age girl, $200/week to babysit Jean and her other kids. This at least allowed her to find another higher-paying job.

She looked for jobs at WorkSource and she didn't have much experience. She went to Goodwill and applied for a job there. She did the job interview at the Goodwill store on

La Brea Avenue. The job interviewer questioned her experience which annoyed her, but she also expected it as she was a long-time housewife.

"Well yeah, I have done theater stage play, performing, and acting. But I did work as a cashier 15 years ago and most recently. I have been cashiering almost five years total."

The job interviewer said, "Okay, we might call you, thank you for coming." But they never did.

She noticed the Apartment owner charged her $20 for the renovation fee and she could disagree with the charge at the HUD meeting. HUD stands for Housing and Urban Development. She never went there before, but she and the other apartment resident showed up and spoke up about the unfair charges to the HUD authorities in the conference room.

"Most of these residents are artists, nurses, actors, waiters, we don't care about the $5,000 worth of kitchen appliances and the new fresh white paint on the wall in the lobby. We aren't making $5,000 a month, there is no way we will be able to afford rent. Why increase the rent, for a doctor to move in?"

After the meeting was over, she visited the department which provided section 8. She filled out an application and was told she will have to be on the waiting list which takes about a year or two. Calista then visited the department which helps provide public housing. She applied and was told she will be on the waiting list. Things were becoming beyond frustrating and stressful, crying herself to sleep some nights as she realized that they might be homeless soon.

Calista was desperate. The rent on her apartment had gone up for the third year in a row, and she could barely keep up with bills as it was. But month after month, she paid it, because where else could she go?

She'd heard that other building owners in her neighborhood were kicking out their tenants and renovating the properties to raise the rent even more. Some of these new apartments were going for triple what she paid each month, and they weren't even that nice!

It made Calista sick to think about losing her apartment—and worse, having to move her kids to a new school district. But another rent increase? She just couldn't afford it.

The HUD dismissed her case, and the apartment owner can charge her $20 for the renovation fee. Calista got frustrated, unwilling to pay $20 for every small and large fix that the apartment desperately needed due to their negligence. She stopped paying her rent in protest and used the rent money to take her kids to Disneyland.

Calista was tired. She was tired of being treated like trash by her landlord, and she was tired of being treated like trash by the world.

She had just lost her job because she always showed up late for work. Jennifer was sick with diabetes. She was waiting for her friend, Diana to come babysit Jennifer at 8 o'clock in the morning. Diana worked as well, but she worked nightshift. But since Calista lost her job, she had to look for another job, after Jennifer becomes well again.

So that added to her problems, her husband Jeff ran away with another woman and was living his best life. Now she was stuck trying to raise their five children alone in a rundown apartment that had rats and mold and leaky pipes—to say nothing of the peeling paint and exposed wires. And now stuck with medical bills to treat Jennifer. Medicaid did help some, but she preferred a specialist who can give Jennifer the best medical treatment. So, she would have to pay out of her own pocket, 100 percent of the payment.

So, when the apartment manager came knocking on her door, demanding his money, Calista looked him right in the eye and said "No."

"I'm not paying you," she said, "because my daughter is sick with diabetes. My child's health is important. My children are my top priorities. And plus, I ain't paying because it is my right to disagree with the rent increase. I don't want to pay the renovation fee."

The apartment manager warned, "I'm just doing my job. I understand your situation. The renovation fee is just $25."

"Yeah, to fix up the apartment building, renovating the lobby, leasing office, the swimming pool area, renovating the apartment units right after the previous tenants moved out, making it nice and pretty for your future rich tenants. And not renovating my apartment unit, I'm not paying it!" Calista slammed the door in manager's face.

And so, she didn't pay. Instead, she chose to give herself and her kids the break they deserved. Going to

Disneyland was a spur-of-the-moment decision, but it felt good because for once, she was in control. It wasn't something she could afford, but for once, Calista felt like she had power over her life again.

After Jennifer's health had gotten better, Calista paid $2,160 worth of Park Hopper tickets for 5 days and she even got a whole house to herself, 3 bedrooms on AIRBNB which was $233 a night. She and her kids were having a blast, finally enjoying a family vacation where they didn't feel stressed or worried or concerned about money. Calista and the kids were riding on rides and eating good fun food, looking at shows, and watching the fireworks popping over the infamous Castle.

After returning home, Calista was ready to take her youngest, Jean, to her first day of preschool. Calista opened the door and as they were leaving the apartment, there was a pink note on the door. It said: "Eviction Notice." She took it down and then walked toward the sickly weak elevators. One of the kids pressed the button while she put the pink letter in her purse, pushing her panic down deep inside.

After dropping off her kids at school, she went to her apartment unit and entered. Then sat in front of the computer, using the internet to search for an eviction attorney. She saw an ad with the 1-800 numbers and felt desperate enough to actually start calling them. She called and they gave her their address and advised her to bring everything she needed, especially the pink "Eviction Notice" paper.

She rode the city bus to Hope and Main Street, walked to the building's door which was on North Pico Boulevard, and she pressed the doorbell which had the label, "1 800 Eviction." A woman answered and Calista talked through the intercom as she looked up at the security camera.

"This is Calista, I called you an hour ago."

The woman told her, "Go around the back, we'll let you in."

So, Calista went up the hilly parking garage and went around the back, and then knocked on the red steel door. The knuckles were in pain because she wasn't sure if they could hear her through a 3 inches cold steel door. The place looked strange for a lawyer's office, but Calista was in no position to turn down the only help she could possibly get. She couldn't afford a lawyer, but she couldn't afford to represent herself either so she had to take whatever would be handed to her.

A man opened the door, "Hi, I'm Josh, Are you...?"

"Yeah, I'm Calista"

"Did you bring your papers?"

"Yes, I did, I have it right here in the folder." She opened the folder and gave him the pink letter. They entered and Josh sat down next to her at a round table.

Reading the pink letter and then he pulled the application up toward him which had laid on the table. Told her to fill it out and made the payment of "$50". She gave him her debit card and he opened the office door and handed the debit card to his assistant before they continued. He sat back down and asked Calista in the nicest of tones, "What happened?"

"I didn't pay the rent because my daughter was sick with diabetes and had to pay medical bills. Plus, I was charged with a renovation fee, and I feel that the apartment people should clean my carpet, paint my wall, and give me a new refrigerator and air conditioner. It is only due to neglect that they must do all this work. They stopped servicing my apartment years ago. Plus, there is a roach problem. It said on the list that I shouldn't have to pay the rent until they give me a new carpet… They never gave me a new carpet before we moved in. Plus, the carpet is black with smog. I won't let my kids sit on the floor and I make them wear slippers in the house, for goodness sakes!"

Josh took notes the whole time and she felt relieved afterward. He seemed optimistic and told her she can go back home now; he'll take care of this. He even offered to contact her via email and phone. Like a miracle, a few days later, the apartment owner was following the court order. The maintenance workers knocked on her door in the early morning on Friday.

Calista opened the door, and they all came in to start shampooing the carpet with their power carpet cleaner. The floor was no longer black, it became tan like when they had moved in all those years ago. Then they sprayed the whole three-bedroom apartment unit with the help of the exterminator to kill roaches and termites. Calista and her kids had to go to the beach and stayed there all day before being put up in a hotel just down the road from their apartment. Just watching the waves and relaxing, sometimes walking a mile along the beach was a perfect day for her and the kids. Finally, something went right for her.

After a day, they came back and put the stuff back in the closet and put the dishes back in the cabinet. They moved the table and chairs and beds back next to the wall after the exterminator told them they could go back to normal. Then the maintenance men came back to install a brand-new refrigerator, stove, and air conditioner. Calista was astonished as they then removed the old wallpaper and painted the wall white, the wall is no longer light yellow. Everything was looking so nice and new.

Calista regretted spending all her money from her savings. Her mother, who is a retired teacher, helped pay the apartment rent, $1,200, plus $20 renovation fee. And when the next month, July came, she paid for the rent, using the Rental assistance from the social services.

Then, she once again met Nathaniel. Unexpectedly in an elevator at the apartment while she was going to job training.

"Hello," he smiled, keeping it friendly when he recognized her out of her office business suit.

"Nice seeing you again," she offered as they were the only ones in the elevator. "How are you?"

"I'm good, got my day off today," he chuckled, holding up his coffee mug. "Going to meet a friend and have some lunch."

"Wow, that's great," she nodded, smiling kindly up at him. "Who is your boss anyway?"

"I'm not allowed to say." He's driving as a chauffeur and, also working as a butler. "I'm not allowed to say his name."

"He must be pretty famous."

The elevator stopped at the third floor, making him chuckle. "This is my floor, nice talking to you again."

"Alright, have a good day," she smiled, waving at him as the elevator closed on her.

The job training went great, she had gotten the nice assistant job in an ad executive office at Universal Studios, which was close enough to the movie business that she thought she might be able to get her foot in.

Things were looking up and improved for both her and her family. But it isn't really enough to pay the living cost. Many businesses hired immigrants for lower salaries, which meant it would be harder to find another job.

Everything was going smoothly when Calista decided to date Nathaniel after knowing him for a few months. She styled her hair, put on makeup, used caramel foundation to cover up her freckled face, and then put on a nice blue dress with gold high heel shoes. She hadn't gone out on a date before she married her husband, Jeff. That was almost 14 years ago.

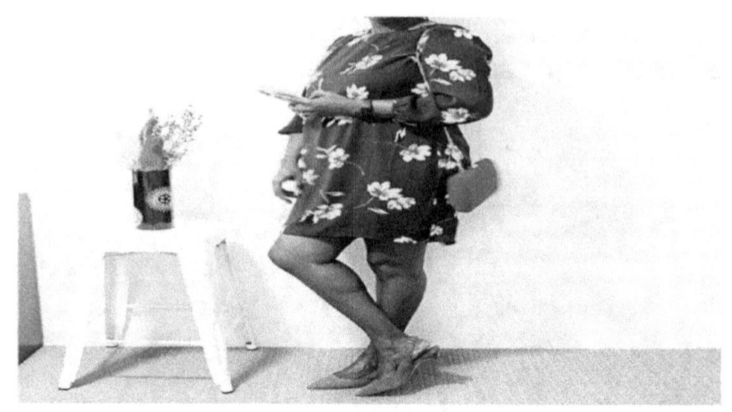

Calista always knew she had options. But how do you know what options are right for you when you've been with the same person for most of your life?

It was strange, getting back into the dating world after being married to one person for so long. Even though Nathaniel always presented himself as a perfect gentleman, it still felt strange going out as a single woman—especially being a single mom with five kids. There are very few men out there who would be willing to take on five kids, she thought.

But despite her fears, Calista felt hopeful about Nathaniel. He made it clear that he would be patient with whatever pace she wanted to set. She also liked that he really seemed interested in getting to know her children as well as her. But even with all this going for him, Calista couldn't shake the feeling that something was off, but she ignored it.

After a few dates with Nathaniel, life finally began to feel good for Calista. She still had a mountain of bills to pay and the stress of juggling five children, but she felt... happy. Nathaniel was so kind and attentive, his eyes glinting with affection whenever he looked at her.

Calista still couldn't believe that Nathaniel had asked her out; she'd always thought boyfriends were something reserved for younger women. With her graying hair and wrinkles from all the stress she had been under, she thought she could not attract any man at all, let alone someone as perfect as Nathaniel.

But as the months passed by and their relationship deepened, Calista began to notice some things about Nathaniel that weren't quite right: he would never let her see where he lived or meet his family, and he seemed evasive whenever she asked him what he did in his free time, which she brushed off too because he was so good with her kids.

After a year went by and it's 2019, Caliste and Nathaniel were boyfriend and girlfriend. They'd been dating and he had been around her and her kids enough to understand the routine. Often, when the kids would bother him enough, Nathaniel offered to buy sandwiches for everyone. At the restaurant, Subway usually, they were ordering sub sandwiches, drinks, and chips. Watching the Sandwich Artist bagging up the sandwiches with chips, Calista's youngest child Jean, wanted the fudge chocolate chip cookie.

As the Sandwich Artist rang up the cashier register machine, it came with $48 total. Nathaniel pulled out his credit card and offered it to the worker.

The worker told him, "No, just slide or chip it in". Nathaniel put the card in the chipper.

Sandwich Artist pressed a few buttons, "It declined. Do you have any other cards or cash?"

Nathaniel answered, "No" As he patted and put his hands in his pants' pockets.

Calista went into her purse, "I'll pay for it." She gave the card to the cashier.

Jennifer knocked down a bunch of small bags of chips on the floor at that moment, making Calista sigh in annoyance.

While Calista and the other children were picking up the chips off the floor and weren't looking, the worker gave her card to Nathaniel. He took it and put it in his back pocket. Then he grabbed the bags of food and absent-minded Calista grabbed the drinks off the counter.

"Y'all, grab the other drinks," she commanded her oldest children, Irene, Tia, and Duane. "Let's go." They walked out the door together.

The rent day came, and Calista gave the check to her apartment landlord at the leasing office.

Then she proceeded to take her son, Duane to the baseball practice which starts after school around 4 pm every Friday.

A week later, the landlord emailed her, saying that the check had bounced. She checked her bank account online and saw there was a negative $1,000. She called the bank to see what was going on with her bank account. The banker told her the money was wired. There was no way that the bank could dispute it so if it was a fraud, her banker offered to send her a new debit card and suggested that she should call the police. Calista called the police, and they only took the report over the phone.

Fearing being evicted, she went to Home Depot and bought a pint of white paint. Then went to her apartment and poured paint over the table. Broke the apartment's door lock. Then she called the rental insurance company to claim that her furniture was vandalized. Before she could file a claim, she needed to call the police first to report it and then tell them how much the table was worth.

Calista's heart raced as she lied to the officers about her furniture being vandalized. She hated that she had to be deceitful, but it was either that or be evicted because there was no other way, she could come up with rent money. She felt like she couldn't catch a break. Any time she got ahead; something would happen.

"Can you describe the vandals?" One of the officers asked her.

"Well..." Calista hesitated, trying to come up with a description. "They were probably wearing masks so I couldn't see their faces."

"Were they white? Black? Asian?"

"I don't know... maybe white."

"How tall?"

"I don't know..."

What if these officers arrested some poor innocent person for vandalism he or she didn't commit just because of her lies? She felt terrible and nervous. Thankfully, the officers didn't suspect a thing and finished writing up the report.

While her kids were busy watching TV, and enjoying the cartoon, the cops were standing nearby, giving her information on where to get a copy of the police report. Then she called back the rental insurance company to let them know that she got the police report and the fake price of the furniture.

Later, she told the apartment landlord that she will get a check soon from the rental insurance company. The landlord, Lucy, told her, that is fine. She'll wait. Within a few weeks, she received a $2,000 check from the mail and road the city bus to the bank. And then she deposited the check at the bank. Waited a few days for the check to clear. She went back to the bank to get the $1,856 money order and then gave it to Lucy for to pay rent. The fee for bounced check and late fee were included.

Calista also told Nathaniel what had happened, which he pretended not to know.

"Yeah, and my bank had to give me a new bank card," she sighed, shaking her head. "New account as well. I also had to change the password to log-into the Bank website… I changed it to Hollywood404. I know I could remember that easily."

The next month came by, she had to go and get a money order since the apartment doesn't accept her checks anymore. She walked her kids to school and went to the bank. She couldn't find her new debit card. The banker asked for her name and driver's license.

The banker looked at the screen, "There is no money in this account, do you have any other bank account?"

She rushed to the social services and asked if they were still paying her.

The case manager said, "No, there had been no changes. Money is going straight to your new bank account." He showed her the account number.

"That's not my bank account."

"Well, you changed it four days ago."

"No, I changed my bank account the week after my bank gave me a new bank account."

"Okay, well, I'll just change it back to your previous bank account. You need to report to the police about this. Someone who has all of your information and social security numbers probably did this."

"Maybe my husband or um," she paused. "My boyfriend." She looked down, hoping it wasn't her boyfriend doing this to her.

A few days later after she walked her kids to school and then dropped them off. Calista walked back to the apartment building. She walked by the apartment leasing office.

The receptionist was sitting at the desk, staring at Calista as she passed by the door. Calista didn't even bother to look at her face.

She came up to the double elevator and pressed the button to go up. Entering the elevator, she rested her forehead against the elevator wall. The elevator opened on the fifth floor, and she walked out of the elevator.

She knew there will be pink paper taped on her door eventually for the world to see. Just a form of humiliation. She took it down and sat on her sofa. She fell into a deep depression. She looked at the bottle of alcohol which was a few feet away on the minibar.

A phone rang, she reached over to pick up the phone which was on the end table next to her.

Nathaniel was on the other side of the phone, "Hey, can you bail me out of jail. I'm sorry for everything, but I don't want to be in this jail cell."

She hung up. She didn't care anymore. As a former housewife and a former stay at home mom, she learned so much about how harsh the world is. She wasn't prepared to be the victim. Now, she really didn't know who to trust anymore. She was an innocent naïve person, at the age 35 and she was really shocked and traumatized. She thought about her children. Couldn't believe she brought her children into this world. She no longer read books about rainbow, unicorn, and other fantasy stories to her kids. She finally took off the rose colored glasses.

Many days passed by, and the apartment had to hire an attorney. She tried to pay her two months' rent, but the apartment wanted to kick her out. She received a letter from the apartment's attorney saying that she must show up for court. Failure to show up, the Judge will give them the right to throw her stuff out. She called the 1-800 Eviction number, and a legal aid picked up.

"Hello? This is Calista Briggs…"

The phone clicked. She had to find a licensed lawyer to help her out. Searching through the internet and then writing down the address.

She walked up to Wilshire Blvd, searching for the address 1930 Wilshire Blvd. She entered the building, looking at the amazing well-decorated Christmas tree in the lobby, she pressed the elevator, and it went up to the 2nd floor. She entered the office, Eviction Net, with a room full of people sitting in the lobby.

She sat in the lobby. There was an overhead TV, but she was staring at the black woman in the wheelchair, wondering if she ever had a disability check to help pay her rent or she couldn't afford the rent with that disability check. Then she stared at the man holding the baby, he was a healthy average looking man, he couldn't get a job, or something happened. She waited nearly four hours.

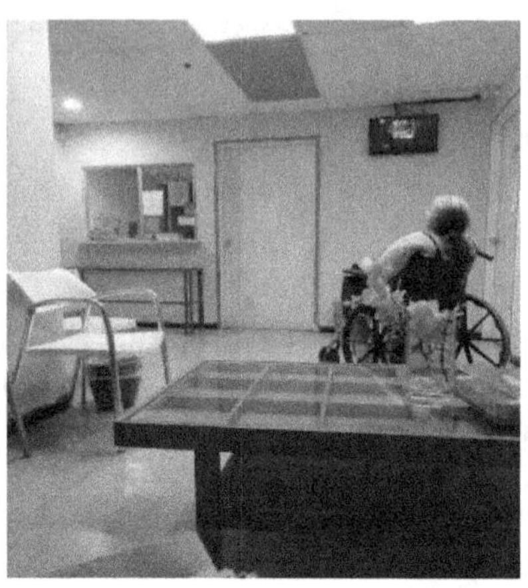

Finally, a receptionist unlocked the door and called out Calista Briggs. The receptionist led her to Mark Strath's office. A hardworking lawyer. He looked a little bit like Ryan Gosling, but older. He did care about people. Fighting for people who were in deep trouble. After usual processing, Calista filled out the application and signed the contract, and then made payment using her debit card. Mark explained that she had to show up to the court, the Eviction Department courtroom. Also, he wanted her to go with him to meet with the Mayor.

"I just need someone like you who can't pay these ridiculous skyrocketing rent. A single mother whose husband left her with five kids. You're a great example. You're not someone who did drugs or has a mental issue. Do you have any mental illnesses? I mean, May I ask that?"

"No, I don't have any mental illness. Well, I am depressed about my situation, but no, I don't have a history of mental illness. You can count depression as a mental illness. I haven't gone to a psychologist or anything like that."

"Well, that's fine, I guess. We can still go see the Mayor. How about Monday, next week?"

"Sure, no problem."

At the Los Angeles city hall, Mark had picked up Calista from her apartment, so they walked toward the building, entered in, and finally sat at the mayor's desk.

"Well, I was thinking you would want to take on the huge job of providing decent, safe, and clean housing for Los Angeles`s poorest citizens," Mark said.

"There isn't enough money," Mayor Ronda explained, though she seemed convinced. "There never has been, and there's even less now. But I can try."

This was one of the reasons Calista hated voting. As she listened to Mayor Rhonda explain the reason there was no money in the budget to help the poor, she got angrier. It wasn't just that she was angry, it was that it made her feel foolish and small. She hated the feeling of being lied to, hated the feeling of having her time wasted by politicians who didn't have the best interests of the people in mind. But the more Mayor Rhonda explained the situation, the more understanding Calista became.

"Well yeah, the apartment I am in, you can turn it into public housing… also the other apartment buildings around it. The people like me that are living in the apartment should stay and pay the rent as we did over 10 years ago. Life was good. It's just sad that we have had to work so hard to get a nice home, but now it seems like it is impossible."

"I get what you're saying. I'll think about it. Thank you for coming in to talk to me." She shook hands with Mark and Calista.

Sachin, a real estate investor, heard that the mayor was planning to take over HUD (Housing and Urban Development) and turn some of the apartment buildings into public housing projects. Sachin of course chose greed over humanity.

A few days later, at her apartment, she sat at the kitchen island counter with her cellphone. "We are planning on having a peaceful demonstration," Calista said after calling Rhonda. "More than 100 people will gather in downtown Los Angeles Saturday to show support for affordable housing. Would you like to join us?"

Rhonda smiled, "That would be great, let me check my schedule, did you say Saturday, that the 15th?"

"Yes, correct."

"I marked my calendar, yes I will come," Rhonda peeked at the calendar on her desk and wrote a note.

"Cool! Thank you, it would mean so much."

As soon as they hung up, Sachin walked into Rhonda's office. Sachin introduced himself and they sat down,

"Do you want people like us here…. The Successful ones? You can have this city with shops, tourists, booming businesses, plenty of funds in your account for community events, and whatever else your city might need. You know, like New York City, people go there because the place has something historical to see. Have you been to New York City?"

"Yes, I have been to New York City."

"Beautiful, right?" he asked.

Rhonda nodded yes.

"Well, why not turn Los Angeles into New York City, with great parks, safe and great neighborhoods, and awesome restaurants. Many wealthy people love living there," he suggested.

"I had a great conversation with the activist Mark Strath and his client Calista Briggs, they brought up some good points and told me that it will help build my resume, to give back to the community and all that stuff."

"Do you want this city to be a shit hole and dealing with people like Calista, 'I have babies, boo hoo'. Look at what they did to the poor Senator in Baltimore, shaming him because his district was drug-filled and poverty and unsafe. It didn't look great on his resume."

On the 15th of March, Sachin took Rhonda out to dinner at a really nice 5-star Michelin restaurant, showing her a stack of money, "Fund for your campaign." She took the money and looked at it.

Calista called Rhonda at the event... but Rhonda isn't answering the phone. She didn't show up to the event that Calista had to organize. That's when she realized something very important: Mayor Rhonda didn't care about anyone but herself and her friends. She just wanted to stay in office, so she could get rich off of all of the bribes she received from corporations for blocking progressive legislation.

The next time there was an election, Calista made sure everyone knew exactly who Mayor Rhonda really was: a self-serving coward who didn't care about anyone.

But Mark Strath showed up and people were cheering. He made a great speech. Thousands of people came instead of a hundred, which made Calista surprised.

Sachin set up an event at the MacArthur Park for the opponents who were against turning apartment buildings into housing projects.

The leader yelled, "We don't want to live next to Trash!! Just go get a job!!!"

A protester yelled, "We don't want our tax money to go to more housing projects!!!

The leader yelled, "We'll just tell the mayor to stop. Enough is enough. Put our money into a big business to create more jobs instead."

The opponents sent a death threat to Calista. Calista feared going out and feared to take her children to school. But she went and walked her kids to school. Two protesters got out of their car and yelled at her and her kids, "Why can't you get a job?" Calista and the kids ran while the protesters chased after them. As Calista and the kids entered the school, the school security guard at the door yelled at the protesters, "You're on school property, get off here!!!"

People treated Calista badly. She feels that it isn't worth it, that the injustice she was trying to fight against would never get solved without money, influence, power and a real chance to form a voice. They will reap what they sow. It got so bad that even residents threw cigarette butts at her window air condition unit.

Rhonda had also ignored Calista's calls again. Rhonda went and celebrated with celebrities at a party with Sanchin.

Calista went to the eviction court with her kids. They sat with other people in the crowded room.

The apartment's lawyers want to talk to Calista with a mediator. The Judge allowed the lawyers to do so.

Calista was leaving the courtroom with Mark Strath, "Y'all sit still, I'll be back soon."

Her kids looked at each other and were obedient, staying out of the way and quiet.

The Apartment's lawyers, Calista, Mark, and the Landlord were standing in the hallway of the court.

One of the Apartment's lawyers asked, "I heard that you have Autism, is that just mild?"

Calista became confused, "What?" She looked at Mark.

"Wait, let me be alone with my client," Mark said to the Apartment's lawyers.

The Apartment's lawyers walked away and sat on a bench in the hallway.

Mark explained to her, "I told them that you have Autism and, so that, the Judge, ummm, you know, can feel sorry for you."

"Okay, well it isn't that severe though. But if it will help, that would be fine."

Mark waved at the Apartment's lawyers to come back. So, they got up and walked toward them.

One of them asked, "Can you feed yourself? If you have a medical record that states your Autism, could you show it to us?"

"Okay, I will get the medical record. It has been a long time ago… like 10 years ago, I don't know if they still have that."

Mark said, "Yeah, she can get those medical records, no problem."

Later, Calista went to the hospital record department and requested a document about her health.

A few weeks later after she got some copies, she showed up at the Eviction legal place on Wilshire Boulevard and sat for hours while her kids were at school. Watching a man eating his boxed dinner, probably got it from a Thai restaurant.

She got up and talked to the young white female receptionist and yelled at her, "Why does this take so long? Why aren't there any more lawyers here? I don't understand. I think it is unprofessional to have all of us here, waiting like this, for hours. Why not give us an appointment instead?"

The other receptionist opened the door and told her, "Mark Strath is ready for you."

Still frustrated, she gave the medical copies to Mark Strath at his office…

Mark wiped his tiring eyes with his right fingers as if he didn't sleep in months.

They sat opposite each other at the table.

Mark smiled, "I heard you in there… see you should do that in the court… but you seem so like, 'okay whatever' in a soft voice. Okay. Here I want you to do, if you see a sign that says, 'Warning, Asbestos on the wall, just look around the building… it could be anywhere. If you don't see that sign. We can tell the court that. Asbestos on walls causes cancer and birth defects, so Apartment buildings are required to show that sign. You moved into that building and didn't know the wall has Asbestos."

**ASBESTOS CONTAINING
MATERIAL EXISTS IN
THIS BUILDING**

"Okay, sure, I will do that."

As weeks passed by, at the courthouse, on Thursday morning… She and her kids stood in a long line, which is out the door to the street. Stood there for 30 minutes.

She and her kids left the line and went to the back of the courthouse and entered through the security gate, putting her purse in the container and rolling it. The security guard scanned her things… to make sure there was no gun or weapon. And they walked through the metal detection. Then they went up the elevator to the Eviction Department's floor.

In the courtroom, her children sat quietly on the bench behind her as she stood next to her lawyer Mark, Landlord, and the apartment's lawyers stood in front of a female blond long hair female Judge who seemed like she was in her 50s.

Mark gave the Judge the medical record and so the Apartment's lawyers argued that Calista has severe Autism, and she wouldn't be able to feed herself and her kids."

Calista burst out, "Do I look like I'm starving? If my kids were starving, they would've been skinny, and the school would've been concerned!"

The Judge agreed to let Calista stay in the apartment, but she must pay the next month's rent... and the court record will be sealed, and nobody will read that she was nearly evicted. "Do we have a deal?" the Judge asked.

Calista nodded her head, "Yes, thank you, your honor."

The landlord spoke up, "That is ridiculous your honor, she owed 4 months' rent. She needs to pay the whole 4 months' rent."

The Judge didn't listen, "Next, who's next?"

The Bailiff pulled up a yellow pad and looked at the list of defenders and plaintiffs, as Calista and Mark walked the aisle toward the exit... Calista waved to her children to get up off the bench. Calista smiled and hugged Mark.

At night at her apartment, sitting on her bed, she thought that the Apartment's lawyers will use her disability against her to the *Department of Child* Protection *Services.* Making it seem like her disability is making her incapacitated. She could lose her kids as well… People may say she isn't fit to be a parent to the kids, since she is unable to take care of herself. Plus she will struggle to pay the rent anyway, why all the stress?"

She sat on her bed, staring out of her apartment's window and thinking about her kids. She knew she couldn't give them much: not the neighborhood they deserved, not the school system they needed, not the family environment she wanted them to have. And now she was wondering if she could even keep them safe.

She didn't want to be here… She doesn't want to deal with this… Her mother offered to pay for the plane tickets. She gave up and put her and the kids' things in storage. Then she and her kids flew to Mississippi to move in at her mother's house.

A few days later, Mark emailed Calista and asked, "Where are you? Calista, get your ass back down here and fight. This city needs you. So, fight!"

Calista responded, "I am not enough…. That city needs people to be more compassionate… more jobs, less Greed, less government… I might as well stay in Mississippi. Los Angeles is hell."

A year later, in 2020, the city was plagued with Covid, homeless, and high rent.

The business owners shut down their stores… won't pay high rent or lease.

Crime rating went up, robberies at the stores…

Walking out with items and rioting over the death of a black man, killed by a white cop.

Young women were prostituting on street corners. The motels were making good money because Johns and prostitutes were renting out the room.

Residents want to vote out Rhonda.

Los Angeles has become a camping ground for the Homeless, with Tents everywhere, even at the park and on the beach at Venice Beach, California. Many residents bought RVs which stands for Recreational vehicles.

Mayor Rhonda stood at the City Hall's balcony.

She jumped and fell on the concrete sidewalk.

The standbys were screaming, "oh my God."

Her suicide was displayed all over the media and the internet.

Sachin lost investment and money... everything crashed down, people weren't renting the apartment, and many moved out. There was ongoing eviction, many tenants were being put out. Had nowhere to go. The tenants were fighting outside the courthouse, against the landlords. The furniture, clothes and things were put out on the sidewalks. And some people were living in tents on the sidewalks.

Now Sachin, a homeless… doing yoga in the middle of the park, shirtless.

Still emailing each other, Calista suggested, "Maybe we need to remove the corrupted government in Los Angeles, even California, and you should run for Mayor… after you win…   I'll probably move back. But anyway… I'm going to focus on my children and their education."

Mark said, "Good idea. Let's Stay in touch."

Mark laid flat on his office's brown couch and finally got some sleep.

ACKNOWLEDGEMENTS

Thank you, God. Thank you, holy spirits. Thank you, everyone who stood by my side. I am grateful for you.

*